Witty and Whimsy Tales
Vol. 1 - Adventure Stories

Namita Das

Ukiyoto Publishing

All global publishing rights are held by
Ukiyoto Publishing

Published in 2023

Content Copyright © Namita Das
ISBN 9789359203287
All rights reserved.
No part of this publication may be reproduced,
transmitted, or stored in a retrieval system, in any form
by any means, electronic, mechanical, photocopying,
recording or otherwise, without the prior permission
of the publisher.

The moral rights of the author have been asserted.
This is a work of fiction. Names, characters,
businesses, places, events, locales, and incidents are
either the products of the author's imagination or used
in a fictitious manner. Any resemblance to actual
persons, living or dead, or actual events is purely
coincidental.

This book is sold subject to the condition that it shall
not by way of trade or otherwise, be lent, resold, hired
out or otherwise circulated, without the publisher's
prior consent, in any form of binding or cover other
than that in which it is published.

www.ukiyoto.com

*For my sweet boy Kuku,
who brings joy, adventure and challenge to my life.*

Contents

Brushstrokes of Magic	1
The Bunny Teacher	8
The Sweet Symphony of Dreams	16
Tuk Tunes & Science Dreams	24
The Great Cookie Catastrophe	31
Magic Beyond the Socks	39
Bonu's Thrilling Delhi Adventure	47
About the Author	55

Brushstrokes of Magic
Unleashing Riya's Whimsical Talent

Riya was a shy and quiet girl who loved to draw. Her sketchbook resembled a zoo of hilarious animals, silly flowers, and wacky landscapes. But she guarded her drawings as if they were top-secret documents. She was convinced that if anyone saw them, they would either burst into laughter or declare her the queen of silliness.

One fateful day, Mr Kumar, the eccentric art teacher, burst into the classroom wearing a polka-dot bowtie and a hat shaped like a paint palette. "Attention, young artists!" he exclaimed, twirling around. "We're on the verge of witnessing some of the most magnificent works of art ever!"

Riya's eyes widened with a mixture of excitement and apprehension. What kind of magical journey involved paintbrushes and canvases?

Mr Kumar announced the unique project: each student had to create a painting of their favourite place and unveil it to the class. Riya's heart skipped a beat. She had always been more comfortable hiding behind her drawings, not displaying them to the world. She wished she could paint herself as an invisible superhero.

Determined to face her fears, Riya painted her secret spot: a hidden pond in the park, where ducks had a knack for comedy and flowers danced to their own beat. With every brush stroke, she couldn't help but giggle at the funny scenes unfolding on her canvas.

On the presentation day, Riya nervously clutched her painting behind her back like a ticking time bomb, ready to explode with laughter. Mr Kumar, with his bowtie now spinning like a whirlwind, called out Riya's name, his voice dripping with anticipation.

Riya shuffled to the front of the class, her knees wobbling like Jell-O. The moment of truth had arrived. With a dramatic flourish, she revealed her painting, and the room fell silent.

Suddenly, a voice from the back of the class broke the silence. "Hey, are those ducks wearing sunglasses?" a classmate exclaimed, pointing at the mischievous waterfowl on the canvas.

Everyone laughed, including Mr Kumar, whose bowtie spun so fast it looked like a helicopter propeller. "Riya, my dear, you have painted a beautiful scene and brought a touch of whimsy to our classroom!" he chuckled.

It was a magical moment of pure joy. Riya's cheeks turned as red as a cherry tomato. She couldn't believe her quirky imagination had made everyone laugh.

From that day on, Riya's artwork became famous in the school, earning her the "Queen of Quirkiness." She embraced her unique talent, sharing her hilarious creations with her parents and friends and even entering them into a prestigious art contest where she made the judges burst with laughter.

Riya had found her magic, and it wasn't just in her ability to see the funny side of nature—it was in the power of laughter and the joy it brought to everyone who witnessed her whimsical art.

The story's moral is: Embrace your unique talents and share them with the world. Sometimes, we may feel afraid or unsure of our abilities, worrying about how others perceive us. However, by overcoming our fears and embracing what makes us unique, we can discover our magic and bring joy to ourselves and those around us. Just like Riya, who found the courage to share her artwork and discovered that her quirky perspective was appreciated and brought happiness to others, the story teaches us the importance of embracing our talents, letting go of self-doubt, and sharing our unique gifts with the world.

Activity Time: Embrace Your Magic and Unleash Your Creativity!

We hope you've enjoyed Riya's delightful journey in "Brushstrokes of Magic." Now, it's your turn to embark on exciting activities to help you embrace your unique talents and discover your magical perspective.

1.   **Magical Nature Hunt**: Step outside and find your very own "magical" spot in nature. Take a photo or draw a picture of what you discover. Don't forget to add your imaginative touches to make it truly enchanting!

2.   **Whimsical Artwork**: Grab your art supplies and create your own whimsical masterpiece inspired by the story. Paint or draw scenes that showcase your unique vision of magic in the world around you.

3.   **Imaginary Duck Adventures**: Imagine the incredible adventures the ducks from Riya's painting might have. Write a short story or draw a comic strip to bring their magical escapades to life.

4.   **Sharing Talents**: Reflect on your unique talents or interests that you haven't shared yet. How could you share your magic with your friends, family, or community?

5.   **Magic in Everyday Objects**: Look around your home for ordinary objects that you can transform into something magical. Draw or craft to bring out their enchanting qualities.

6. **Create a Comic Strip**: Make your own comic strip or storyboard that captures Riya's journey's key moments and personal growth.

7. **Story Remix**: Give the story a fun twist! Imagine if Riya's painting had a different magical element. How would the story unfold?

8. **Art Show and Tell**: Organise a mini art show with your friends or family. Display your artwork inspired by the story and share the magical elements you've added.

9. **Design Your Own Mentor**: Get creative and design your quirky and eccentric mentor character. What would their outfit and personality be like?

10. **Nature Journaling**: Start a nature journal where you can sketch and write about the fantastic things you observe in the natural world, just like Riya.

Remember, your unique talents and perspectives are waiting to be explored. Embrace your magic like Riya did, and let your creativity shine!

The Bunny Teacher
A Tale of Hopping Misunderstandings and Heartwarming Lessons

Once upon a time, a mischievous young boy named Rohan lived in a vibrant town. Rohan had an uncanny ability to add a dash of laughter and wit to every situation. One sunny morning, as he strolled through the bustling streets, he overheard his teacher, Mrs Gupta, conversing with another teacher.

"Guess what, my friend! I have some thrilling news to share. I'm going to have a baby!" Mrs Gupta exclaimed with glee.

"Oh, my stars! Congratulations! That's absolutely wonderful!" the other teacher replied.

Rohan's eyes widened with curiosity and excitement. He wanted to inform his friends about Mrs Gupta's baby immediately. However, amid all the commotion, a twist of fate intervened. Rohan misheard the word "baby" and instead thought Mrs Gupta said "bunny."

"Hey, listen up, everyone! Mrs Gupta is going to have a bunny!" Rohan excitedly whispered to his friend Rajesh during recess.

"A bunny? Seriously? How utterly delightful!" Rajesh exclaimed, his eyes twinkling with joy.

"Oh, indeed! I can imagine Mrs Gupta bringing the bunny to class and letting us have wild hopping races," Rohan giggled mischievously.

Rohan and Rajesh, united by their love for bunnies, made it their mission to spread the news of Mrs Gupta's upcoming bunny adventure.

"Psst! Have you heard the hop-tastic news? Mrs Gupta is bringing a bunny to class!" Rajesh whispered conspiratorially to their friend Priya in the courtyard.

"No way! A bunny? How adorable!" Priya exclaimed, her face lighting up with excitement.

"Oh, absolutely! I can already picture Mrs Gupta and her bunny hopping around, painting beautiful pictures during art class," Rajesh added, painting a whimsical image in their minds.

Emboldened by their playful tales, the trio set out to share their enchanting rumours with their other friends.

"Guess what, my friends? Brace yourselves for the magical news! Mrs Gupta will make a bunny perform flips and tricks during music class!" Priya whispered, her voice filled with anticipation, to their buddy Alok.

"Wait, seriously? A bunny? That's bunny-sational!" Alok burst into laughter, unable to contain his excitement.

"Absolutely! Just imagine Mrs Gupta and her bunny doing the tango while playing the harmonium!" Priya exclaimed, their imaginations running wild with amusing possibilities.

The whispers and giggles continued, each tale becoming more whimsical and extraordinary.

"Psst! Prepare to be amazed! Mrs Gupta will make a bunny talk and sing like a Bollywood superstar during lunch break!" Alok whispered with a grin to their friend Rina.

"You've got to be kidding me! A bunny? That's simply unbelievable!" Rina's eyes widened with wonder and disbelief.

"And picture this, Rina, Mrs Gupta will teach the bunny classical Bollywood dance moves while it sings melodious tunes!" Alok added, their laughter echoing through the corridors.

The anticipation reached its peak as the children eagerly awaited Mrs Gupta's arrival the next day. The classroom buzzed with excitement, each child hoping to witness the extraordinary talents of Mrs Gupta's bunny.

Finally, Mrs Gupta entered the classroom, her eyes sparkling with joy. The children held their breath, ready to be amazed.

"Good morning, my dear students! I have the most wonderful news to share with all of you. I'm going to have a baby!" Mrs Gupta announced, her face beaming with happiness.

Silence fell over the classroom as confusion washed over the children's faces. The fantastical bunny tales they had spun came crashing down.

They exchanged sheepish glances, realising their wild imaginations had led them astray. With a mixture of amusement and embarrassment, they apologised to Mrs Gupta and congratulated her on her baby.

That day, they learned a valuable lesson: not to believe every tale they heard and to be cautious before spreading rumours. From that day forward, they never forgot that their beloved teacher, Mrs Gupta, was not a bunny magician but a human being with a baby on the way, ready to embark on her extraordinary adventure.

The story's moral is to not believe everything you hear and to avoid spreading rumours without checking the facts. It highlights the importance of being cautious and verifying information before jumping to conclusions or spreading potentially false or misleading stories. The children in the story learned the value of being mindful of the accuracy of the information and the consequences of letting their imaginations run wild without proper verification. The story also teaches the importance of showing respect and consideration towards others, as the children realise their mistakes and apologise to their teacher for their wild bunny tales.

Engage with the Story: Fun Activities for Kids!

Congratulations, you've finished reading "The Bunny Teacher: A Tale of Hopping Misunderstandings and Heartwarming Lessons"! But the adventure doesn't have to end here. Keep the excitement alive with these engaging activities that will let your imagination soar and reinforce the valuable lessons you've learned:

1. **Draw Your Own Bunny**: Grab your crayons and paper! Draw your very own version of the bunny from the story. Make it as unique and imaginative as you can. What tricks can your bunny perform?

2. **Create a Classroom Newspaper**: Become a reporter for the day! Imagine you're writing a newspaper article about the bunny rumours that spread like wildfire in the story. Draw pictures, write headlines, and share the scoop with your friends.

3. **Act Out the Story**: Gather your friends or family and act out your favourite scenes from the story. Who will play Rohan, Rajesh, Mrs Gupta, and the bunny? Get ready to bring the tale to life!

4. **Fact-Checking Challenge**: Test your detective skills! Have someone give you statements to fact-check. Are they true or false? Like in the story, this will remind you to verify the information.

5.   **Imagination Showcase**: It's your time to shine! Like Rohan and Rajesh did, come up with your own creative rumours. Share them with your friends and family in a fun and imaginative showcase.

Remember, stories are not just meant to be read – they're meant to inspire, teach, and make you smile. So, dive into these activities and let the magic of "The Bunny Teacher" brighten your days. Happy learning, exploring, and laughing!

The Sweet Symphony of Dreams

Embracing the Sweetness of Life Through Passion and Dreams

Meera was a young girl who lived in a vibrant land where the streets were coloured with festive shades, and the spices' fragrance wafted through the air. Meera had a magical touch when it came to baking, and her heart beat faster for the aroma of freshly baked cakes than for the sound of a Bollywood dance number.

Meera dreamed of becoming the reigning cake baker queen and winning the prestigious Mithai Mela (Sweet Festival). This competition was open only to the finest bakers, who faced judges with palates more refined than a chef's knife and eyes as sharp as a hawker spotting a prospective buyer.

Day and night, Meera tirelessly practised her craft, experimenting with flavours rivalling a masala chai's complexity. She skillfully adorned her cakes with intricate patterns inspired by henna art and shimmering with edible gold. She mixed cardamom with chocolate, saffron with vanilla, and mango with coconut, creating fusions that delighted taste buds.

One auspicious day, an invitation arrived for Meera, inviting her to showcase her talent at the grand Mithai Mela. Excitement coursed through her veins like the beat of a dhol drum during a wedding procession. This was her chance to prove herself and bring joy to dessert lovers across the country.

Determined to create a masterpiece, Meera decided to bake her signature cake—a towering creation of rose-flavoured sponge layers filled with pistachio cream and adorned with delicate strands of silver vark. The kitchen became a whirlwind of spices and sweetness as Meera poured her heart and soul into every batter and frosting.

With her cake nestled securely in a traditional brass carrier, Meera arrived at the Mithai Mela, where the air buzzed with excitement and the tantalising scent of sweets lingered. She gazed at the other bakers, their creations as diverse as the cultures of India, and a twinge of nervousness tickled her senses. But Meera's determination remained unshakable, like a sturdy banyan tree in a gusty monsoon.

The judges, esteemed chefs known for their discerning palates, glided through the rows of tables like royalty. Their eyes sparkled with anticipation as they approached Meera's creation. Her heart pounding like a dhol, Meera greeted them with a warm smile, ready to infuse her passion into their taste buds.

One judge, his moustache twirled like a Bollywood hero, asked Meera about the inspiration behind her cake. She replied playfully, "Well, I asked the mischievous kitchen deities for a pinch of magic and a sprinkle of nostalgia, and voila! This cake was born, carrying the flavours of our rich traditions."

The judges chuckled, their eyes glimmering with curiosity as they sliced into the cake with the precision of a samosa cutter. The flavours exploded on their tongues like fireworks during Diwali, and their faces lit up with delight.

After tasting all the delectable creations, the judges gathered on a stage, the atmosphere brimming with anticipation. The audience held their breath as if waiting for the climax of a thrilling Bollywood movie.

One judge stepped forward, his voice resonating like a melodious tabla beat. "Ladies and gentlemen, we have unanimously decided after much savouring and deliberation."

Meera's heart fluttered like a butterfly's wings as the judge continued, "The winner of the Mithai Mela, the queen of confectionery, is none other than... Meera!"

Ecstatic cheers and applause erupted from the crowd, creating a symphony of joy. Meera's eyes widened with disbelief, and she could hardly contain her excitement. She gracefully made her way to the stage, crowned with a shimmering sugar crystal tiara and presented with a golden trophy.

As she stood on the stage, bathed in the crowd's adoration, Meera's mind wandered to the lessons she had learned. She realised that her success wasn't just about winning accolades; it was about sharing love, culture, and the flavours of her art. It was about the joy on people's faces when they tasted her creations and the moments of togetherness they brought.

With a renewed sense of purpose, Meera vowed to continue her baking adventures, infusing her cakes with the warmth of hospitality and the spirit of celebration. She would bake to win competitions and create memories that would be cherished for generations.

And so, Meera's journey as the queen of cake baking began, spreading sweetness and happiness to every corner of the country. From the bustling streets of Mumbai to the serene ghats of Varanasi, her cakes became a symbol of unity, reminding people that no matter their differences, there was always room for a slice of cake and a shared moment of joy.

And they all lived happily ever after, enriched by Meera's delectable creations and the sweet connections they forged. The end... or the beginning of a new chapter in Meera's delightful baking tale.

The story's moral is that while pursuing our passions and dreams is essential, it is equally crucial to strike a balance and not lose sight of the other joys and experiences life offers. The story reminds us that there is more to life than just achieving success or winning trophies. It encourages us to appreciate the moments spent with loved ones, find joy in simple pleasures, and embrace life's broader aspects beyond our specific pursuits. It teaches us to savour the sweetness of our accomplishments and the moments of connection and celebration arising from them.

Activity Time: Sweet Adventures Await!

We hope you've enjoyed Meera's heartwarming journey in "The Sweet Symphony of Dreams." Just like Meera, you, too, can embark on exciting activities to help you explore your passions and appreciate the sweetness of life. Here are some delightful activities for you to try:

1. **Baking Bliss**: With the help of a grown-up, dive into the world of baking! Create your own cupcakes or cookies and experiment with different flavours and decorations. Let your imagination run wild, just like Meera did.

2. **Dream Cake Creation**: Imagine and draw your dream cake on paper. Think about the flavours, colours, and decorations that make your cake extraordinary and uniquely yours.

3. **Decorate and Delight**: Finish your creative juices by decorating plain cupcakes or cookies with icing, sprinkles, and colourful fruits. Have a blast making your very own edible masterpieces!

4. **Share Family Recipes**: Talk to your family members, especially grandparents, about their favourite traditional recipes. Create a unique family cookbook with these cherished culinary treasures.

5. **Discover Henna Art**: Learn about the fascinating world of henna art. Design your own henna-inspired patterns on paper using coloured pencils or markers.

6. **Explore Your Passions**: Like Meera, explore your interests! Whether painting, dancing, playing music, or another hobby, spend time doing what you love.

7. **Create Precious Moments**: Plan a fun family game night, movie marathon, or picnic. Cherish the time spent with your loved ones and create lasting memories.

8. **Strive for Balance**: Make a collage that represents balance in life. Cut out pictures from magazines or print images to show various activities that bring joy and fulfilment.

9. **Write Your Story**: Like Meera, imagine a character who follows their dreams and learns important life lessons. Write a short story that showcases their journey.

We hope these activities add fun and inspiration to your days. Just remember, like Meera, you have the power to create your own sweet symphony of dreams. Enjoy your adventures, and keep spreading joy!

Tuk Tunes & Science Dreams

An Unlikely Journey to Friendship

Once upon a time, two strangers had the same destination in mind. One was a young man named Ravi, who was a passionate musician. He carried his guitar, a backpack, and a heart full of aspirations. Ravi dreamt of going to Mumbai, where he hoped to make it big as a renowned singer. The other was a young woman named Priya, a talented scientist. She had her laptop, a suitcase, and a groundbreaking research project. Priya aimed to present her findings at a prestigious conference in Mumbai.

Living in Bangalore, they faced the challenge of insufficient funds for plane tickets. So, they turned to the internet for carpooling options and eventually found each other. Ravi and Priya decided to share the expenses of the journey and take turns driving. They met at a bustling parking lot, where Ravi had his old car waiting. It was a colourful, decorated auto-rickshaw, commonly known as a tuk-tuk. Priya was intrigued by its charm but also concerned about its reliability. On the other hand, Ravi found Priya's reserved demeanour to be intriguing but initially thought she might be too serious.

After introducing themselves, they loaded their belongings into the tuk-tuk. They set out on their adventure, hoping to reach Mumbai in four days. They soon realised they had pretty contrasting personalities. Ravi enjoyed listening to lively Bollywood tunes and singing along. At the same time, Priya preferred the calming melodies of classical music, lost in her thoughts. Ravi loved sharing humorous anecdotes and stories, while Priya was more interested in intellectual discussions and acquiring knowledge. Ravi enjoyed making stops at interesting places to capture memories. Priya was determined to maintain a steady pace and save time.

They seemed to argue about everything - the music, the speed, the route, the food, the accommodations, the weather, the sights - even the colours of their surroundings. Their constant disagreements annoyed each other so much that they regretted having embarked on this journey together. They wondered how they would endure four days in such close quarters.

However, as they journeyed through the diverse landscapes, they witnessed awe-inspiring sights. They marvelled at the Taj Mahal, awestruck by the timeless beauty. They explored the mystical forts of Rajasthan, where they felt transported back in time. They visited the serene backwaters of Kerala, where they connected with nature's tranquillity. They encountered the vibrant culture of Varanasi, where they experienced spiritual enlightenment.

And amidst these incredible experiences, they also discovered more about each other. They learned that Ravi was a boisterous singer and a versatile musician who could play any tune effortlessly. Also, Priya was a studious scientist and a brilliant researcher with innovative ideas about sustainable technology. They discovered Ravi's compassion and kindness, as he would stop to help the needy along their journey. Priya witnessed Ravi's adventurous spirit, always keen to explore new places and try new things.

As they spent time together, they realised they had more in common than they initially thought. They both shared a love for travel and discovering new places. They were driven by ambitious dreams and determined to positively impact society with their talents.

Surprisingly, they found themselves developing a fondness for each other. They began appreciating each other's music, discussing the essence of Indian melodies and Western tunes. Priya started enjoying Ravi's entertaining stories, while Ravi admired Priya's inquisitive mind and her desire to understand the world better. They even found a middle ground where they could occasionally stop at intriguing places and continue their journey without significant delays.

As they progressed, they evolved into close friends. They laughed together, shared their dreams, and supported each other's goals. They reached Mumbai just in time for their appointments on the fourth day. They parked the tuk-tuk near the Gateway of India, where they bid each other farewell with a warm hug. They wished each other good luck and promised to stay in touch.

As they walked away, mixed emotions filled their hearts - happiness for the remarkable journey they shared and sadness at the thought of parting ways. They were uncertain if their paths would ever cross again. Still, one thing was sure: they had created memories that would remain etched in their hearts forever.

The story's moral is that friendships can be formed in unexpected and challenging situations. Despite their differences and initial disagreements, Ravi and Priya discovered they had more in common than they thought. Their journey together taught them to value their different gifts, and they grew as people. The story emphasises the importance of open-mindedness, understanding, and finding common ground with others, even when they seem very different from ourselves. It teaches us that embracing diversity and valuing each other's strengths can form meaningful connections and create lasting friendships that enrich our lives.

Engage and Explore: Fun Activities for Young Adventurers!

Congratulations, young adventurers, on completing the exciting "Tuk Tunes & Science Dreams: An Unlikely Journey to Friendship" journey! But the adventure doesn't have to end here. Let's keep the spirit alive with these engaging activities that celebrate the themes of the story:

1. **Design Your Own Tuk-Tuk**: Unleash your creativity by crafting your very own tuk-tuk masterpiece! Decorate it with musical notes, scientific symbols, or designs representing your interests and dreams.

2. **Bollywood Dance Party**: Turn the music and groove to some Bollywood beats! Channel your inner Ravi and dance like nobody's watching. Share your dance moves with friends or family and spread the joy.

3. **Collaborative Storytelling**: Collaborate with a friend or family member to write a story. Like Ravi and Priya collaborated, you'll learn how combining ideas can lead to exciting and imaginative tales.

4. **Science Fun at Home**: Become a mini scientist and try a simple science experiment at home. Create a mini volcano eruption, make slime, or explore the magic of a rainbow with water and light.

5. **Share Your Talents**: Showcase your unique talents to friends and family. Whether singing, drawing, telling

jokes, or performing magic tricks, sharing your abilities is a beautiful way to connect and have fun.

6. **Explore Landmarks**: Discover interesting landmarks in your city or neighbourhood, just like Ravi and Priya did on their journey. Take a trip with your family and learn more about the world around you.

7. **Cooking Creations**: Team up with a grown-up for a tasty treat. Baking involves science and creativity – from measuring ingredients precisely to decorating your delicious masterpiece.

8. **Write Letters of Friendship**: Express your gratitude and friendship by writing letters or drawing pictures for your pals. Share something you learned from the story and tell your friends how much you appreciate them.

Remember, the magic of "Tuk Tunes & Science Dreams" is about embracing differences, finding common ground, and celebrating the beauty of friendship. Have a blast with these activities, and let your imagination soar, like Ravi's tunes and Priya's scientific discoveries!

Keep exploring, dreaming, and spreading kindness, young adventurers!

The Great Cookie Catastrophe
A Sweet Tale of Friendship and Crumbs

Once upon a time, in a land filled with sugar and laughter, there were two mischievous pals, Kabir and Alok. They were practically joined at the hip, always up to some wild antics. Soccer matches turned into chaotic dance parties, bike rides became epic races against imaginary creatures, and movies were always accompanied by outrageous commentary. But their greatest shared love was undoubtedly chocolate chip cookies.

One sunny day, with mischievous grins, Kabir and Alok decided to embark on a culinary adventure and bake their own cookies. Armed with a recipe that promised cookie bliss, they gathered ingredients and donned their imaginary chef hats.

With a sprinkle of laughter and a dash of silliness, they mixed the dough, giggling as flour flew in every direction. Kabir, the fearless risk-taker of the duo, spiced things up by adding an extra pinch of excitement. Little did he know that the recipe didn't call for excitement but for baking soda! Nevertheless, they placed the cookie dough in the oven and anxiously awaited the arrival of their mouthwatering treats.

Suddenly, a cloud of smoke emerged from the oven, twirling like a clumsy ballerina. The boys' eyes widened in horror as they witnessed a tray of cookies resembling blackened hockey pucks.

"Uh-oh!" exclaimed Kabir, his face turning as pale as unbaked dough. "I think we've got a cookie catastrophe on our hands!"

Alok, ever the quick thinker, jumped in. "We can't blame the oven for being a hot mess. Or maybe it's just trying to toast our friendship to perfection!"

Their eyes met, and a spark of humour broke through their disappointment. They burst into laughter, realising they were in this cookie chaos together.

However, their laughter quickly gave way to a blame game as they each tried to find the culprit behind the cookie catastrophe. Accusations flew faster than a cookie dough tornado.

"You must have set the timer wrong!" Kabir said, pointing an accusatory finger at Alok.

"No way! Maybe you put too much baking soda instead of sugar!" Alok retorted.

Their argument escalated, with each boy blaming the other for every cookie catastrophe imaginable. It got so heated that they decided to take a break from each other, slamming their doors like cookie monsters.

Days passed, and Kabir and Alok were lost in their cookie kingdoms, baking and concocting luxurious treats. They built higher and higher fences between their yards as if their delicious creations needed extra protection from the other's taste buds.

But then, one bright morning, the aroma of freshly baked cookies tickled their noses simultaneously. Curiosity overpowered their stubbornness, and they both peeked over their high fences, their eyes widening at the sight before them.

"Hey, Alok, your cookies have grown into skyscrapers!" Kabir shouted, unable to contain his amusement.

Alok's eyes sparkled mischievously. "Well, Kabir, your cookies have been on a diet! They're so tiny; they must have been baked in the land of leprechauns!"

They couldn't help but compare their cookie creations, each more extravagant than the last.

"No way!" Kabir yelled back. "My cookies are the best!"

They held up their plates and compared their cookies. They both looked good, but they were very different.

"Your cookies are too crunchy!" Alok exclaimed.

"Your cookies are too soft!" Kabir replied.

They couldn't resist the temptation any longer. With plates held high, they marched toward the fence, ready to declare their cookie superiority. But as they stood face to face, their rivalry was sheer ridiculousness.

Cookie insults flew across the fence like playful butterflies. They tossed cookies at each other, laughing as they tried to dodge the sugary missiles. Cookies whizzed through the air like tiny UFOs, leaving trails of crumbs behind.

Soon, their yards resembled a battlefield of baked goods, with chocolate chips as ammunition and frosting as camouflage. The Great Cookie War had begun!

But as the last cookie flew through the air, landing with a splat on the ground, Kabir and Alok suddenly realised the magnitude of their sweet showdown. The frowns turned into giggles, and their eyes widened at the mess they had made.

"What on earth have we done?" Kabir gasped.

Alok scratched his head, trying to hide a sheepish grin. "I guess we got a bit carried away, huh? We should have been baking bridges instead of cookies!"

They exchanged apologetic glances, a sprinkle of remorse coating their hearts. With a genuine sorry, they reconciled and realised how silly their quarrel had been. They learned that friendship was the sweetest ingredient of all.

Together, they cleaned up the remnants of their Great Cookie War, transforming their yard into a sugary wonderland again. The fence, once a symbol of separation, was dismantled brick by brick, freeing their yards and friendship.

From that day forward, Kabir and Alok shared everything, from soccer matches to bike races and their delicious creations. They even invented a new game called "Cookie Catch," where they tossed cookies to each other and caught them in their mouths, creating a sugary symphony of laughter.

As their laughter echoed through the neighbourhood, the scent of freshly baked cookies drifted in the air, a reminder of the Great Cookie War that had transformed into an even more incredible friendship.

The story's moral is that friendship and shared experiences are more important than winning or being right. It teaches us that arguments and disagreements can lead to unnecessary rifts, and it's important to apologise, forgive, and find common ground. The story encourages us to value our friendships, communicate openly, and embrace the joy of sharing and laughter together.

Activity Time: Sweet Adventures Await!

Are you ready to embark on your own sugary escapades, just like Alok and Kabir? After enjoying "The Great Cookie Catastrophe," why not dive into fun activities to bring the story's lessons to life? Here's a batch of exciting activities to keep the laughter and learning rolling:

1. **Cookie Creations**: Gather your ingredients and try baking your chocolate chip cookies. Teamwork makes the dream work, just like with Alok and Kabir!

2. **Design-a-Cookie**: Get your creative hats on and decorate cookies with all the colourful fixings – sprinkles, frosting, and chocolate chips. Let your imagination run wild!

3. **Friendship Bracelets**: Craft unique friendship bracelets for your pals, a heartwarming gesture inspired by the story's heartwarming end.

4. **Role Play Reunion**: Gather your friends and enact scenes from the story. Take turns being Alok and Kabir as you practice communicating and resolving conflicts.

5. **Build a Cookie Fort**: Channel your inner architect! Use cardboard, markers, and other craft materials to construct your cookie fortress.

6. **Nature's Cookie Hunt**: Head outdoors on a nature scavenger hunt. Collect leaves, twigs, and stones to craft your own "cookie" creations in the great outdoors.

7. **Measuring Madness**: Learn some kitchen math! Follow a simple cookie recipe, measuring ingredients just like a baking pro.

8. **Draw Your Cookie War**: Put your artistic skills to the test. Draw your version of the Great Cookie War with flying cookies, messy yards, and giggles galore.

9. **Pen a Sequel**: Let your imagination take the reins and write a sequel to Alok and Kabir's adventure. What comes next in their tale of friendship?

10. **Collage of Friendship**: Create a collage that celebrates the spirit of friendship using magazines, newspapers, and craft materials.

11. **Storytime Spectacle**: Share your storytelling prowess. Recount "The Great Cookie Catastrophe" in your own words to friends and family, adding your personal touch.

12. **Discussion Delight**: Gather in a circle and discuss the story's themes of forgiveness and friendship. Share your thoughts on how you can apply these lessons to your own life.

Are you up for the challenge? Choose your favourite activity or try them all to keep the cookie-filled adventure alive. Remember, just like Alok and Kabir, the best stories are the ones you create and share with your friends!

Magic Beyond the Socks
Mohan's Cricketing Adventure

Once upon a time, in a lively village lived a boy named Mohan who had an unbeatable passion for playing cricket. He was a cricket prodigy, consistently hitting boundaries and quickly taking wickets. He possessed a cherished pair of socks that he believed brought him incredible luck. These socks were adorned with colourful patterns of elephants and peacocks, symbolising good fortune and grace.

One fateful day, Mohan's mischievous younger sister, Madhu, decided to play a prank on him. She stealthily sneaked into his room and swiped the lucky socks, leaving a note saying, "To the socks' new owner—Madhu the Mischief Maker." Mohan was devastated when he discovered his beloved socks missing. He knew he couldn't perform his cricketing feats without them.

Determined not to let his spirit waver, Mohan hatched a clever plan. He rushed to his grandmother, known for her sage advice and ancient wisdom. After narrating the tale of his missing socks, she smiled mischievously and said, "Oh dear Mohan, the magic is not in the socks but within you. All you need is a little imagination and belief."

Inspired by his grandmother's words, Mohan decided to create his own lucky charm. He found a pair of plain white socks and, with a twinkle in his eye, painted them with vibrant colours, intricate henna designs, and symbols of victory. In his excitement, he chanted a playful rhyme:

Socks, socks, bring me glory,
With you, I'll create my own story.
No matter the challenge, no matter the strife,
I'll unleash my cricketing skills and bring cheer to life!

With his newly crafted socks on his feet, Mohan joined his friends on the cricket field. Bowling his first delivery, he felt a burst of energy surge. The ball whizzed through the air, deceiving the batsman and hitting the stumps. The crowd erupted with joy, chanting his name. Mohan realised that the magic he sought was not in the socks but in his confidence and determination.

Match after match, Mohan's skills shone brightly. He played great shots, took spectacular catches, and led his team to victory. His friends marvelled at his talent and wondered how he had become even better without his original lucky socks.

One day, as Mohan returned home, he noticed his younger sister, Madhu, hiding something behind her back. She wore a mischievous grin that betrayed her secret. Curiosity piqued, and Mohan approached her cautiously. Madhu's playful giggle filled the room as she revealed the missing socks, freshly washed and ironed.

Mohan's eyes widened in astonishment. He realised that his sister, though mischievous, had taught him a valuable lesson. It wasn't the socks themselves that held the magic, but the belief and determination he carried within. He hugged Madhu tightly, thanking her for the unexpected surprise and her playful prank.

From that day forward, Mohan cherished his original lucky socks not as a source of magic but as a reminder of the bond he shared with his sister. He continued playing cricket with gusto, dazzling the crowds and inspiring other young players to believe in their abilities.

And so, the legend of Mohan, the cricket superstar, spread far and wide. His colourful socks became a symbol of the magic that lies within every young cricketer's heart. They served as a reminder that no matter their challenges, they could conquer them with determination, a sprinkle of imagination, and unwavering self-belief.

The moral of the story is that true magic lies within oneself. It is not external objects or superstitions that determine our success or abilities but our confidence, determination, and belief in our capabilities. The story teaches us that we can overcome obstacles and achieve greatness with imagination, hard work, and self-belief. It encourages children to trust in themselves, embrace their unique talents, and realise that they have the power to make their dreams come true.

Unleash Your Own Magic!

Congratulations on completing Mohan's inspiring adventure! Now, it's time to discover and embrace your magical abilities. Like Mohan, you have a world of potential and imagination waiting to be unleashed. Here are some exciting activities to help you connect with the story's themes and embark on your unique journey of self-belief:

1. **Create Your Magical Charm**: Grab some plain white socks or fabric, along with colourful markers, paints, and craft supplies. Design your very own lucky charm, just like Mohan's socks. What symbols and designs represent your own magic and confidence? Let your creativity soar!

2. **Magic Rhyme and Chant**: Learn Mohan's magic rhyme in the story. Now, come up with your own memorable rhymes for different situations. Whether before a big test, a dance performance, or even trying a new sport, your rhyme can be your secret source of courage.

3. **Sports and Fun Day**: Gather your friends and family for a mini sports day! Play cricket or any other sport you love. Remember Mohan's determination and self-belief as you engage in friendly matches and showcase your skills.

4. **Share Family Stories**: Sit down with your family and share stories about times you faced challenges, believe in yourselves, and succeeded. This is a beautiful way to bond and draw inspiration from each other's experiences.

5. **Draw Your Adventure**: Grab your favourite art supplies and recreate a scene from your imaginary adventure. Let your creativity flow as you draw yourself to achieving something extraordinary, just like Mohan did in his cricketing journey.

6. **Unleash Your Imagination**: Set aside time to imagine various scenarios where you could use your magical abilities – from scoring goals in soccer to acing a math problem. Remember, your imagination knows no bounds!

7. **Sibling Collaboration**: Team up for a creative project if you have siblings. Write a short story together, create a piece of artwork, or plan a fun family activity. Working together can create its own kind of magic.

8. **Reflect and Believe**: Take a moment to reflect on a challenge and how you conquered it. Think about your inner strengths and the magic that helped you succeed. Believe in yourself just as Mohan did!

9. **Discover Indian Culture**: Learn more about Indian culture by exploring symbols like peacocks and henna designs. Draw these symbols or discover their meanings to gain insight into different cultures.

10. **Magic Show and Tell**: Prepare a "magic show and tell" where you share something that makes you feel confident and magical. Let your unique magic shine, whether it's a talent, an object, or a story you've written.

Remember, just like Mohan, you have magic within you. Embrace it, believe in yourself, and let your imagination soar. Your journey of self-discovery and self-belief is about to begin – enjoy every magical moment!

Happy exploring, young adventurers!

Bonu's Thrilling Delhi Adventure
Unveiling New Colors of Joy!

Dear Laddu,

I trust this letter finds you in good spirits. I miss you dearly and eagerly await the day we can reunite. How are things back home? How's Amma and Appa and our little buddy, Biscuit?

I have some thrilling news to share with you. You'll hardly believe what unfolded yesterday. It was an adventure unlike any other in my life!

Remember how I mentioned I'm staying in Mumbai with Aunty Leela and Uncle Raj? Their home is near this colossal marketplace that divides the city into two sections. One is called South Mumbai, and the other is North Mumbai. They say this marketplace was built ages ago and intended to preserve cultural distinctions. Some still believe in its significance, while others view it as a relic.

Aunty Leela and Uncle Raj are kind and attentive but also relatively conventional. They're not keen on going out for enjoyment or engaging in anything unconventional. They spend their days watching TV, reading the newspaper, and discussing current affairs. The market's historical significance and cultural implications frequently occupy their conversations. They have me follow a disciplined routine, consume nutritious meals, and focus on my studies.

They discourage me from playing with toys, games, or comics, citing them as trivial or excessively commercial.

So, yesterday, I decided to venture out alone and explore the city solo. I was curious to uncover the North Mumbai side of things. I longed to have fun, make friends, and maybe even stumble upon hidden treasures.

I dressed warmly in a jacket, hat, muffler, gloves, boots, and a backpack. I packed sandwiches, cookies, juice, a torch, a map, a compass, a pocket knife, and a camera. I also took Biscuit's collar and ID tag in case I lost or sought companionship.

Waiting for Aunty Leela and Uncle Raj to be preoccupied in the kitchen, I slipped out the door and headed outside. It was a chilly, overcast day, but my enthusiasm overshadowed my discomfort.

I strolled through the streets, observing the architecture, vehicles, and people. Everything appeared rather sombre and guarded. Faces lacked smiles, laughter, or songs, and pedestrians hurried with their gaze fixed downward.

I empathised with them, yet I was equally intrigued. What lay beneath their apparent unhappiness? What secrets were they guarding? What fears lingered?

I resolved to uncover the truth.

I followed signs directing me toward the market. It was an immense stone marketplace stretching across miles of the cityscape. It bore decorative motifs, vibrant colours, and intricate designs. It was like a piece of history coming alive and a mystery to be unravelled.

I felt a mix of apprehension and courage. I was determined to unveil the enigma.

I searched for a way to cross unnoticed. I spotted a gap in the barricade near a bridge over a river. Someone had seemingly cut through it using wire cutters.

Carefully, I squeezed through the opening, praying I wouldn't draw attention.

I emerged on the other side.

What met my eyes was beyond my wildest expectations.

It was like a whole new world.

Colours were vivid, and life was effervescent. Markets bustled with shops, cafes, theatres, and parks. Flowers and trees bloomed, and birds and butterflies danced in the breeze. Some people laughed, sang, and danced without inhibition.

Their joy was infectious.

Their freedom was palpable.

And I was joyful.

I was free.

I yearned to be part of it all.

I wandered around, absorbing the vibrant surroundings. I purchased sweets from a street vendor who gave me a knowing smile. I watched an animated film at a theatre surrounded by childlike wonder. I revelled in a playground with swings, slides, and carousels. I struck up friendships with local kids who invited me to their celebration.

They shared cake, ice cream, and laughter.

They embraced me with warmth.

And, Laddu, at that moment, I felt truly alive.

I look forward to sharing more stories and experiences when we meet again.

Yours eagerly,

Bonu

The story's moral can be summarised as follows: Embrace curiosity and adventure, even in unfamiliar situations, as they can lead to unexpected and joyful discoveries. Sometimes, breaking away from routine and trying new things can bring excitement, happiness, and valuable experiences that enrich our lives. Finding a balance between responsibility and exploration is crucial, allowing ourselves to step out of our comfort zones and enjoy the world's wonders.

After the Adventure: Let's Keep the Fun Going!

Congratulations, young adventurers! You've travelled alongside Bonu as he discovered the magic of curiosity, friendship, and exploring the unknown. But the adventure doesn't have to end here. We've prepared some exciting activities for you to enjoy after reading "Bonu's Thrilling Delhi Adventure." Let's dive in:

1. **Colourful Adventure Map**: Design your very own adventure map like Bonu! Use your favourite colours, markers, and stickers to mark the places you'd love to explore.

2. **Exploration Collage**: Get creative with a collage that shows the two sides of your city – one ordinary and the other bursting with colour. Cut out pictures from magazines or draw your own to capture the atmosphere.

3. **Treasure Hunt**: Gather your friends or family and organise a treasure hunt at home or in your backyard. Create clues or a simple map to lead them to hidden treasures.

4. **Design a Playground**: Imagine your dream playground, like the one Bonu found. Draw swings, slides, and all the fun features you'd love to have in your perfect play area.

5. **Write a Letter**: Grab some paper and write a letter to a friend or family member about your exciting adventures

or dreams. You can even write a letter from Bonu to his friend, sharing his new experiences.

6. **Cultural exploration**: Learn about Delhi, where Bonu's adventure occurred. Discover its landmarks, culture, and vibrant markets, and share what you've learned with your friends and family.

7. **Create a Playlist**: Put together a playlist of songs that make you feel curious, adventurous, and joyful – just like Bonu on his adventure.

8. **Dress-Up Adventure**: Dress up as an explorer and reenact scenes from the story. Grab hats, scarves, and backpacks, and let your imagination take you on a new adventure.

9. **Draw and Describe**: Draw a picture of the colourful side of the city from your imagination. Then, write a short description of what you see, hear, and feel in that vibrant world.

10. **New Friend Collage**: Create a collage featuring diverse faces and personalities, just like the friends Bonu made at the birthday party. Celebrate the importance of friendship and embracing differences.

Remember, the joy of exploring and creating is endless. Keep your curiosity alive, and keep dreaming big. Your adventure awaits – who knows where your imagination will take you next? Have a blast with these activities, and continue spreading the magic of Bonu's thrilling adventure!

About the Author

Namita Das

Namita Das, a literary enchantress, crafts tales that captivate both young and old. Her narratives brim with humour, warmth, and imagination, enriched by her insights from being a child counsellor and psychology scholar. Namita's accolades and recognition shine bright as a versatile author, adept blogger, and creative force. The spotlight fell on her with "The Mogra Flowers", featured by the Commonwealth Foundation. At the same time, her blog "Mother and Mind" imparts wisdom on child and educational psychology.

Hosting the beloved podcast "Witty and Whimsy Tales," Namita whisks young minds to enchanting worlds. From the endearing "Keen Little Kuku" to the uproarious "Who

Ate Our Food? " her bookshelf is a treasure trove of diverse wonders.

Namita Das is synonymous with literary brilliance, laughter, and the magic of storytelling. Immerse yourself in her artistry, share her journey, and let her weave laughter, inspiration, and connection into your life. Embark on the voyage through the enchanting universe of Namita Das today.

www.ingramcontent.com/pod-product-compliance
Lightning Source LLC
LaVergne TN
LVHW041549070526
838199LV00046B/1879